Illustrations: Ann de Bode
Original title: *Altijd moeten ze mij hebben*
© Van In, Lier, 1995. Van In Publishers, Grote Markt 39,
2500 Lier, Belgium.
© in this edition Evans Brothers Limited 1997
(world English rights excluding the USA and Canada)
English text by Su Swallow

Reprinted 1999

First published in Great Britain by
Evans Brothers Limited
2A Portman Mansions
Chiltern Street
London W1M 1LE

Printed by KHL (Singapore)

0 237 51754 X

British Library Cataloguing in Publication data.
A catalogue record for this book is available from the
British Library.

HELPING HANDS

IT'S ALWAYS ME THEY'RE AFTER

ANN DE BODE AND RIEN BROERE

Evans

Evans Brothers Limited

Peter is lying in the middle of his room.
He looks around.
His bed has gone, and his chair, and the cupboard.
The toys have all gone, too.
For six years, almost all his life,
this room has been his nest.
And now, he's leaving it. He is moving
from the country to the town.

Peter watches the removal men.
They come into the house empty-handed.
They go out with their hands full.
There are six of them, all working hard.
They hurry to and fro like ants.
Like ants, but as big as bears and as strong as giants.
Giantantbears, thinks Peter.
That's a good word I've just made up!

Peter thinks of Simon. Simon is his best friend.
It will be strange not to see him every day.
It was very hard saying goodbye.
They looked at each other in silence for a while.
Then Simon said, 'When we're grown up,
we'll live in the same village again.'
'Next door to one another,' said Peter.
And they shook hands. Very slowly and thoughtfully.

'Is it far now?' asks Peter.
'Another hour at least,' answers Dad.
They are following the removal lorry.
'Is everything in there?' asks Peter.
'Yes,' says Mum. 'Everything we have is in there.'
Everything? Peter can hardly believe it.
'Stay close to the lorry, then, Dad,' he says.
'If we lose it, we won't have anything left.'

Two hours later they arrive.
The new house is big, with trees all around.
And it's old, old and beautiful.
Peter looks at the top window.
His new room is behind that window, he knows.
It's twice as big as his old one,
and it's all just for him.
Peter thinks his house looks as good as a castle.

This is fun, eating on the floor!
The man next to Peter takes out his sandwiches.
Goodness, what a feast! He's got nearly
a whole loaf of bread.
And the man takes huge bites.
Peter does the same.
'Peter!' says Mum crossly. 'Eat properly.'
Peter can't answer. His mouth is full of food.

'They will take your things up first, Peter,' says Dad.
'Then you can start sorting out your room.'
Peter watches as his bed is taken up in bits.
Then the boxes with his toys.
Now he can't wait to get into his new room.
Moving house is exciting.
Everything looks different.
Even your toys seem like new.

Before Peter starts to unpack,
he wants to show Tiger his new room.
Tiger is his favourite cuddly toy.
Which box might he be in?
In less than ten minutes, the floor is covered in toys.
But where is Tiger?
Surely he hasn't been left behind?

Peter opens the last box,
and finds two shiny black eyes looking up at him.
'Tiger!' he shouts happily, and gives him a hug.
Tiger is so small that he just fits in Peter's hand.
'Peter!' calls Mum. 'Tea's ready!'
'Coming,' calls Peter,
and jumps over a pile of toys.

'You've been upstairs a long time,' says Mum.
'I expect you've put everything away by now?'
Peter gulps his tea.
'Um...well...not really,' he mumbles.
'There are still some things on the floor.'
'Don't worry about that,' says Mum.
'You can go outside for a while.
I'll put away the rest.'

Peter walks down the road.
As he turns a corner he bumps into a boy.
'Look where you're going,' says the boy crossly.
He glares at Peter. His hair is spiky like a hedgehog.
Peter doesn't say a word. He holds on to Tiger.
'Aha! A cuddly toy, eh?' the boy says
with a nasty smile. He grabs Tiger, throws him down
and tramples all over him.

The little group moves off without a word.
Peter waits until they've turned the corner.
Only then does he dare to pick up Tiger.
His favourite toy is ruined.
He's torn and dirty,
and his tail is hanging on by a thread.
Peter's eyes fill with tears.

It's Peter's first day at his new school.

He knows straightaway that he's not going to like it here.

It's not a bit like his old school.

The books are different, and the sums.

'Do you know the answer?' asks the teacher.

But Peter doesn't remember a thing.

Twenty hands or more go up.

Peter feels as though he is the most stupid child in the class.

'Eighteen plus four,' says the teacher.
'How many does that make, Peter?'
Sums over ten, thinks Peter.
I haven't learnt that yet.
'Forty,' he guesses.
The boy in front bursts out laughing.
He turns round
and Peter sees who it is.

At break time, a whole group goes up to Peter,
with hedgehog in the lead.
'Our sums are hard, aren't they?' he says.
'Yes,' says Peter, who thinks the boy is being nice.
'Well we learnt them ages ago,' the boy laughs.
Peter says nothing. He stares at the ground.
Suddenly the hedgehog punches him.
'Silly twit,' he shouts, and walks off.

From then on, all the group pick on Peter.
He tries hard to keep out of their way,
but they always know where to find him.
It's worse at break time and after school.
Then everyone has a go at him.
It gets worse every day.
It's always me they're after, Peter thinks sadly.
If only I was brave enough to fight back.

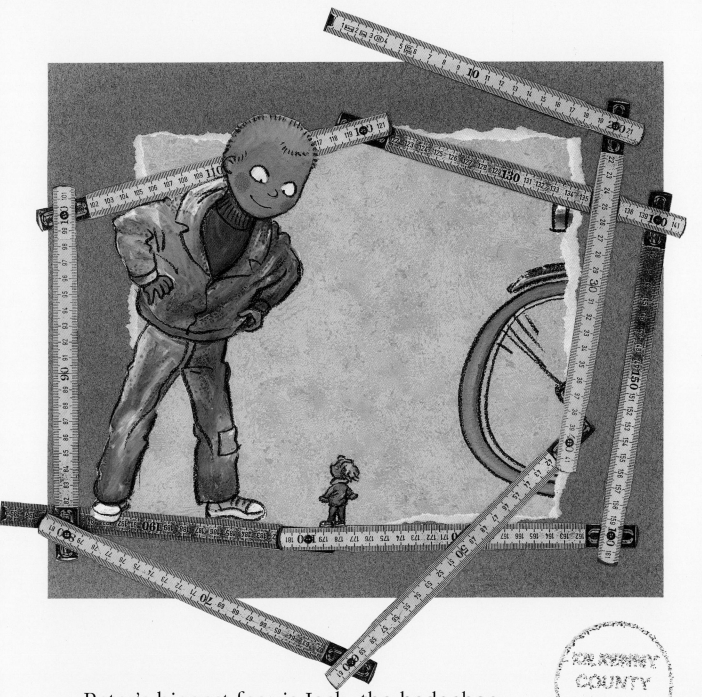

Peter's biggest fear is Jack, the hedgehog.
Jack pesters him when no one is around.
The teacher doesn't notice anything wrong.
And his mum keeps saying,
'Why don't you go and play with your friends?'
I don't have any friends, Peter thinks.
But he doesn't say anything.

In dreams, everything is possible.
In Peter's dreams, Tiger is the biggest
tiger in the world. Peter rides on his back.
Suddenly he sees a little boy with spiky hair.
'Hey, Jack,' Peter cries.
When Jack sees Tiger, his eyes nearly pop
out of his head and he runs off as fast as he can.

In three bounds, Tiger is beside Jack.
Jack is so frightened that even his hair quivers.
Tiger bares his pointed teeth.
His roar rolls round like thunder.
Jack trembles like a leaf.
Now he knows what it's like to feel afraid.
In his dream, Peter wants to laugh out loud.
It even makes him wet his pyjamas.

Oh dear! This wet patch is not just in his dream.
It's real! His trousers are wet,
and the sheet, and the mattress.
What should he do? Call Mum or Dad?
Maybe he'd better change the sheets himself.
Then Mum would be proud of him.
So in the middle of the night Peter strips the bed.
He puts the pile of laundry in a corner.

Mum comes in and sits on the bed.
'What's the matter, Peter?
I know something is wrong. Tell me.'
So Peter tells her everything.
About the hedgehog, and the others.
When he's finished, he feels much better.
'Tomorrow we'll both talk
to your teacher,' says Mum.

Next day, Mum talks to the teacher.
Then the teacher talks to Peter.
'I will try to make sure this never happens again.
But you must promise me that
if anyone does bother you,
you will come and tell me. You will, won't you?'
Peter nods. He will do anything the teacher asks.
As long as this bullying stops.

The bullying does stop, at least in school.
But outside school, Jack is still after him.
Then one day, Peter comes home beaming.
Jack is ill.
Now, the boys in the group play with Peter.
Peter hopes the hedgehog will be ill for a long time.
Mum can't believe it.
Peter's always in a hurry to go out to play.

'I've got an idea,' says Mum. 'You can have a party,
for your new house. You can invite who you like.'
Jack will be better soon, thinks Peter.
Then no one will come.
'And why don't you invite Jack, too?' says Mum.
'I daren't. Anyway, he's ill.'
'Well, just take the invitation to his house.
I'll come with you,' says Mum.

Peter thinks, if Jack sees Mum with me,
he'll laugh at me.
'Can you hide here?' he says.
'Then I'll know you're near, but Jack won't.'
Mum sighs, but she understands.
'All right,' she says
and crawls into the bushes.
'That's fine,' says Peter. 'Just wait there.'

Peter thinks Jack's mum looks very nice.
Not the sort of mum to have a bully for a son.
'Hallo,' he says. 'I've come to ...'
'Oh how kind,' the lady says.
'You've come to see Jack. You know,
hardly anyone comes to play with him.'
I'm not surprised, thinks Peter.
I'll just give the invitation to Jack, then I'll go.

'Look darling,' says Jack's mum. 'A visitor.'
Jack sits up in bed. He looks dreadful.
His face is covered in red spots.
His eyes are full of tears. This isn't a fierce hedgehog,
it's an unhappy monkey!
Peter looks round the room. There's a shelf
full of cuddly animals, and boxes of toys.
It's a room just like his own.

Peter sits on the edge of the bed. Jack looks worried.
Something is rustling under the bedclothes.
Peter puts his hand in to see what it is.
A plastic sheet!
Jack still sleeps with a plastic sheet!
Jack looks straight at Peter. His face has gone very red.
Well, well, thinks Peter. So this is the terrible Jack!
But he says nothing. And Jack is glad.

Jack shows Peter his stamp album.
'That's a good one,' says Peter.
The two boys are sitting together like old friends.
'I think I'll collect stamps, too,' says Peter.
'Here,' says Jack. 'You can have this one.
I've got two anyway.'
Who would have expected this from Jack?
Peter almost forgets how he used to scare him.

Poor Mum! Peter has forgotten all about her.
She is still waiting out in the cold.
A man with a dog walks past.
'Are you alright?' he asks.
A lady in the bushes, you don't see that every day!
'Oh yes, I'm fine,' says Mum, a bit embarrassed.
'I was just looking for something.'
She gets up quickly and walks away.

It's Peter's party today. The house is very busy.
Most of the guests bring a little present.
Jack is last to arrive. He has a parcel too.
Peter tears off the paper.
'Oh, Jack,' he cries. 'It's great!
It's the best cuddly toy ever.
You know what? I'll call it Tiger.'
And Peter feels happier than he's been for a long time.